Shearing the sheep.

Solomon's hind leg kicked out, right into the sharp blade of the shears. The young ram squealed. Blood fell onto the white fleece.

"Oh!" Hannah cried, startled.

Suddenly everything was noisy and confused. "Baa!" bawled the ram in pain. Other sheep bleated in answer, milling around in their stalls. Solomon was struggling to stand, while Jemmy tried to hold him down and Father looked for a rag to wrap around the injured leg.

"Here," said Hannah, ripping a strip of cloth from the hem of her dress.

She put her arms around the injured sheep's neck. "There, there," she said softly in his ear. "It's all right. Father will take care of you."

Solomon seemed to understand. Slowly, very slowly, he quieted down and let Father bandage the leg.

Father looked at Hannah. He didn't smile very often, but he was now.

"Daughter," he said, "you surely do have a way with animals."

**The Pioneer Daughters series
by Jean Van Leeuwen**

Hannah of Fairfield
Hannah's Helping Hands
Hannah's Winter of Hope

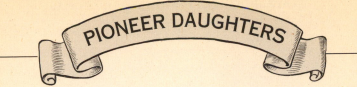
PIONEER DAUGHTERS

Hannah's Helping Hands

JEAN VAN LEEUWEN

PICTURES BY DONNA DIAMOND

PUFFIN BOOKS

To my aunt, Ruth Charlton, of Fairfield
—J.V.L.

PUFFIN BOOKS
Published by the Penguin Group
Penguin Putnam Books for Young Readers,
345 Hudson Street, New York, New York 10014, U.S.A.
Penguin Books Ltd, 27 Wrights Lane, London W8 5TZ, England
Penguin Books Australia Ltd, Ringwood, Victoria, Australia
Penguin Books Canada Ltd, 10 Alcorn Avenue, Toronto, Ontario, Canada M4V 3B2
Penguin Books (N.Z.) Ltd, 182-190 Wairau Road, Auckland 10, New Zealand

Penguin Books Ltd, Registered Offices: Harmondsworth, Middlesex, England

First published in the United States of America by Phyllis Fogelman Books,
an imprint of Penguin Putnam Books for Young Readers, 1999
Published by Puffin Books,
a division of Penguin Putnam Books for Young Readers, 2000

1 3 5 7 9 10 8 6 4 2

Text copyright © Jean Van Leeuwen, 1999
Illustrations copyright © Donna Diamond, 1999
Jacket illustration copyright © Harry Bliss, 1999
All rights reserved

THE LIBRARY OF CONGRESS HAS CATALOGED THE PHYLLIS FOGELMAN EDITION AS FOLLOWS:
Van Leeuwen, Jean.
Hannah's helping hands / by Jean Van Leeuwen ;
pictures by Donna Diamond.—1st ed.
p. cm.
Summary: In 1779 in Fairfield, Connecticut, Hannah and her family try to
maintain a sense of normalcy as the Revolutionary War rages around
them, threatening to destroy their way of life.
ISBN 0-8037-2447-0
1. Connecticut—History—Revolution, 1775–1783—Juvenile fiction.
[1. Connecticut—History—Revolution, 1775–1783—Fiction.
2. United States—History—Revolution, 1775–1783—Fiction.]
I. Diamond, Donna, ill. II. Title.
PZ7.V3273Har 1999 [Fic]—dc21 99-17173 CIP AC

Puffin Books ISBN 0-14-130500-2

Printed in the United States of America
Book design by Stefanie Rosenfeld

Reading level: 2.7

Acknowledgments

I am grateful to Barbara Austen and Bill Stansfield of the Fairfield Historical Society for reading my manuscript for historical accuracy. Their comments and suggestions were most helpful. I also appreciate the help of Margaret Vetare, Althea Corey, John Fox, and Joanne Lieboff at Van Cortlandt Manor and Joe H. Plummer of Muscoot Farm. And I am especially indebted to the recollections of Joseph Plumb Martin, a Connecticut soldier during the Revolution, as set down in *Private Yankee Doodle*. Finally, special thanks to my husband, Bruce Gavril, for his patient tasting of many trial batches of johnnycake.

About the Author

Jean Van Leeuwen is the highly acclaimed author of many picture books and novels for young readers. Her previous works of Americana include *Going West*; *Across the Wide Dark Sea*; and *Bound for Oregon*. She is also the author of *Two Girls in Sister Dresses*; *Blue Sky, Butterfly*; *Dear Mom, You're Ruining My Life*; and the best-selling Easy-to-Read books about Oliver and Amanda Pig. With the Pioneer Daughters series, Jean Van Leeuwen continues her tradition of stories that expand her readers' views of themselves and their world.

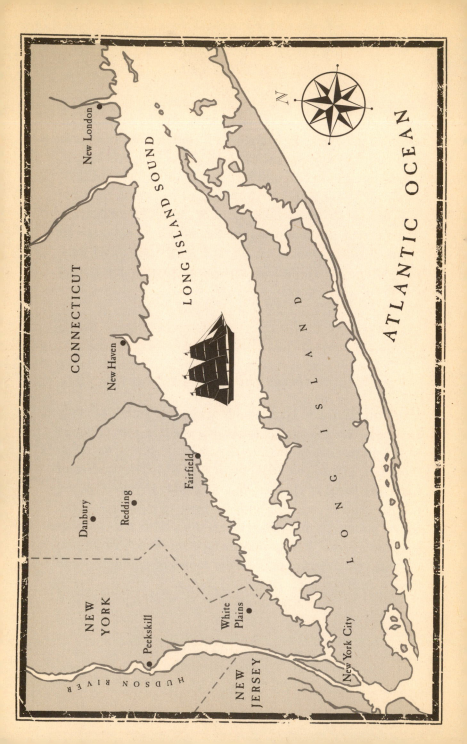

Chapter 1

Hannah heard the birds singing the moment she woke up.

Spring is come, they seemed to say, *I'm so happy!*

Outside her window the sun was peeping through a cloud of new white blossoms on the pear tree. New soft-green leaves waved against the sky. And out in the barn, new spring lambs were waiting.

"Spring is come. I'm so happy!" Hannah sang to herself as she hurried downstairs to help with breakfast.

But her smile faded as soon as the family sat down to eat.

"Today," said Mother, "we start the spring-cleaning."

Hannah knew that meant hard work. Mother always insisted on a clean house. Everything had to shine. So each spring she took the whole house apart and cleaned it until all the winter soot and smoke and dirt was scoured away.

"Jemmy," Mother said, "I'll need your help as well as the girls'."

Jemmy frowned down at his plate. Hannah, sitting next to him, heard him mutter under his breath, "Women's work."

"What's that?" Father looked up from his fried eggs and bacon.

"Nothing." Jemmy dared not talk back to Father. But Hannah knew what he was thinking. Ever since their oldest brother, Ben, had gone off to fight the British two years ago, twelve-year-old Jemmy had tried to take his place. He wanted to be out in the fields helping Father with the planting, as Ben would be.

Or helping Father in his clock-making shop, as Ben would be.

"It will only be for a day or two," Mother told him.

"Can I help too?" asked seven-year-old Jonathan. "I am strong."

"Of course." Mother smiled at him. "We couldn't do it without you."

For two long days, they all worked. They washed windows. They took down beds and carried them outside. They scrubbed floors. They cleaned out fireplaces and whitewashed floors and brought the beds back inside.

"She has no mercy," complained Jemmy, when Mother finally let him rest. His face was covered with soot, his straw-colored hair streaked with whitewash.

Hannah looked at Rebecca, and they both burst out laughing.

"Now you see how easy women's work is," said Hannah.

Finally Mother set Jemmy free. He looked as

if he had just escaped from jail as he quickly disappeared around the barn.

But spring-cleaning wasn't finished yet. The next morning Hannah helped take all the bedding off the bedsteads. Then she and Rebecca carried the feather-filled ticks, used as mattresses, and pillows outside to air in the April sun.

"Now for the washing," said Mother.

They gathered up sheets and pillowcases and brought them outside, where the large iron kettle and oak washtubs were waiting. Then the carrying began. Back and forth they went from the rain barrel behind the house to the tubs, carrying heavy pails of water. Jonathan tried to help, but he could only carry half a pail. And he spilled half of what he carried.

"Fifteen," counted Hannah, her arms aching.

"Sixteen," said Rebecca.

"Seventeen," said Jonathan. But just then he tripped over a stool leg and all his water spilled onto the ground.

He looked up at Hannah, fighting back tears. "Sixteen," he said sadly.

Laughing, she pulled him to his feet. "Come, let's try again."

When the tubs were filled, into the soapy water went the sheets. Hannah and Rebecca rubbed and scrubbed. Then Mother took over. She boiled the sheets in the kettle, stirring them with her long washing stick. Then out they came into the rinse water. And, last, they had to be wrung out.

Soon Hannah's back was aching. She tried not to think about it. What could she think about instead?

"I wonder," she said out loud, "what Ben is doing right this minute."

Mother stopped her stirring. Her gray eyes looked suddenly sad. "I wonder that often," she said softly.

It had been seven months since Ben had been home on leave. And nearly two months since they'd had a letter from him. Then he had

been in winter camp at Redding, in their own state of Connecticut. Where was he now?

"Why doesn't he write to us more?" asked Hannah.

"You know why," answered Rebecca, pushing wisps of pale yellow hair under her cap. At fifteen, she was taller than Mother and looked just like her. "The army is always on the move. And after Ben writes a letter he must find someone to carry it all the way to Fairfield."

Hannah knew that. But if only Ben could write a tiny letter saying he was all right.

"A letter will come," Mother said firmly. She always believed that the best things would happen.

It was late afternoon when they finally finished the washing.

"I'd say we have done a good day's work," said Mother.

Hannah looked around the yard. Spread out in the grass, over bushes, on the garden fence, were all the clean sheets. Bright splashes of white puffing out in the breeze. Like clouds come down to earth, she thought. She had to smile.

But she groaned at Mother's next words.

"Tomorrow," she said, "we will start the ironing."

All the next day Hannah lifted the heavy irons out of the fire. By the end of the day, the fresh linens were folded and put back into chests and drawers.

Finally it was time for the last cleaning job, scrubbing the kitchen floor.

"May I help?" asked Hannah eagerly. This was her favorite chore.

On their hands and knees, Mother and Hannah scoured the wooden floor with sand. Every grease spot, every candle drip had to be scrubbed away.

This was not the part Hannah liked.

Little by little, the hard grains of sand wore away the stains and the floor turned a clean, even white. Of course, Mother had to inspect it.

"You missed a grease spot over there," she pointed out.

This was not the good part either. Back Hannah went on her knees.

But at last Mother was satisfied. She handed Hannah a bowl of white sand from the nearby shore. "Do a neat job now," she said.

This was the part Hannah had been waiting for.

Carefully she spread the sand in an even layer. It would help keep the floor clean by taking up spills. Then, with a broom, she made patterns all around the edges: swirls and curls and feathery loops. Finally, she took a thin stick of wood from the woodbox. What design would she draw this time?

Flowers, Hannah thought. Spring flowers.

She drew daisies around the fireplace, and here and there a bluebird. This was such fun! Now what should she put in the middle?

There was a knock at the door. Hannah hurried to open it before anyone could spoil her sand pictures.

A thin, ragged man stood on the doorstep. A soldier, she saw. But his blue coat was torn and his stockings and britches muddy. He looked so tired he could barely stand.

"Come in," said Mother, behind Hannah.

The soldier sank down gratefully in a chair. Hannah poked up the fire, and soon Mother was handing him a warm cup of chowder.

It wasn't until he finished eating that the soldier finally spoke.

"Thank you, ma'am," he said. Then, reaching into his knapsack, he took out a folded paper with a wax seal and handed it to Mother.

A letter! From Ben! It must be.

Did the soldier know Ben? Was he all right? Where was he? Hannah's mind swirled with questions. But it was not her place to ask them, she knew.

Gently, Mother questioned the soldier. His name was Elijah Perry. Yes, he had seen Ben in New London a week ago and he seemed well. New London was another town along the shore. Ben was still in Connecticut then.

The soldier was not from Ben's regiment. That was all he knew. Mother invited him to stay, but he was eager to move on.

"If I keep walking, I may reach my father's farm before dark," he said.

As the soldier trudged on down the road, Mother placed the letter on the table. "Father will read it aloud at supper," she said.

The whole family leaned forward in their chairs as Father broke the seal on Ben's letter. As usual, he did everything slowly, with great care. He fitted his spectacles onto his nose. He unfolded the paper and smoothed it out.

Hannah thought she would burst from so much waiting.

At last Father began to read:

Honored Father:
Please forgive my not writing of late. I was down with a fever for three weeks, too

weak to lift a pen. But I am some better now and on the march again. Thank you for the shirts you sent in February. They fit just right. I have been carving trinkets to sell for extra bread. Traded a whistle to the sergeant for a new handkerchief.

My love to all the family,
Your dutiful son, Ben

Hannah could see Ben whittling by the campfire, just as he used to at home. Making things from scraps of wood, like the beautiful lamb he had carved for her. She smiled at the thought.

But when she looked up, she saw that Mother was not smiling. Her face looked pale in the firelight.

"A fever," she repeated.

Daniel, thought Hannah. A little shiver touched her spine.

Ben's friend Daniel had died of a fever in army camp a year ago.

Chapter 2

The letter was put away now, in the leather-covered box where Father kept his Bible. But Hannah had read it so many times, she knew it by heart.

Ben had had a fever. He was better now, and marching again. The soldier had seen him and said he seemed well. Everything was all right, Hannah told herself. Still, she couldn't help feeling a little prick of worry.

Mother said nothing more about it. She just worked harder than ever. She kept discovering a few more things to clean.

"Why, we forgot the candlesticks," she said. As Mother polished the dull brass to a bright shine, Hannah thought she was rubbing away her worries.

Mother seemed more cheerful a few days later as she helped Hannah and Rebecca get ready for another spring chore: picking the geese. Twice a year the girls penned up the small flock of geese. Then, one by one, they caught them and plucked out their soft feathers to fill pillows and feather beds.

"You must wear your oldest clothes," Mother reminded Hannah. She handed her a linsey-woolsey dress that Hannah hadn't worn for months. It was made of linen and wool and once, when it had been Rebecca's, had been bright red. But now it had faded almost to gray, and was much too small.

"I can hardly move," complained Hannah.

"Nor can I." Rebecca was wearing an old dress of Mother's and a handkerchief on her head to keep the feathers out of her hair.

Mother smiled. "You two make quite a pair," she said.

She gave them aprons to wear, old stockings to pull over the geese's heads so they wouldn't bite, and a basket to hold the feathers.

Poor geese, Hannah thought, as she scattered a line of corn to coax them into the pen. They didn't know what was about to happen to them.

When the geese were inside, she and Rebecca each chose one. Quickly they drew the stockings over the geese's heads. Then, sitting on the ground, they held the legs tight with one hand while pulling out feathers with the other.

Hannah's goose didn't like this at all. It kicked and squawked.

"There, there, goosey," Hannah soothed it, until slowly it quieted down.

Goosey. That was Ben's old nickname for Hannah. He called her that because he said she was always poking her nose into things.

Rebecca's goose kept struggling. Mud streaked her apron. Downy feathers missed the basket and flew into the air. Both girls started to sneeze.

"Don't you think this is the worst job in the world?" Rebecca asked.

Hannah looked at her, surprised. Even though it was dirty and messy and she felt sorry for the poor geese, she liked being outside. And she always liked being with animals. She shook her head. "My worst job is my sampler."

Sewing seemed so dull to Hannah, so much the same. But every girl was expected to make a sampler, to show how well she could do all kinds of stitches. She had chosen the shortest verse for hers: "In Adam's fall, we sinned all." Even so, at ten years old, she still hadn't finished it.

"I could help you," Rebecca offered. She was good at all the things Hannah wasn't—sewing, spinning, weaving—and always so good-natured too.

"I wish you could." Hannah sighed. She

knew Mother would say it had to be her own work.

Putting the sampler out of her mind, she talked to her goose.

"Just a little longer," she whispered, stroking its neck. As she plucked out feathers and dropped them in the basket, a poem popped into Hannah's head.

"Don't be sad, my little goose," she said. "We'll put your feathers to good use."

Rebecca smiled. "I like that," she said. Soon they had made it into a song.

"Don't be sad, my little goose," they sang to the tune of a church hymn. "We'll put your feathers to good use."

The singing seemed to calm the geese. The plucking went faster. It wasn't long before the basket was nearly full. And only two more geese remained.

Hannah caught hers, and slipped the stocking over its head. But as Rebecca tried to do the same, the cranky old gander snapped at her.

"Ow!" cried Rebecca, letting go of him.

The gander honked and flapped his wings. Rebecca jumped up and chased after him. "Hannah, help me!"

Hannah left her goose to chase the old gander. Around and around the pen they went. At last they had him cornered.

"It's all right," Hannah said in her most soothing voice. "Hush now."

For a moment she thought she had quieted him. Then the old bird hissed at her. "You can't fool me," he seemed to say. And he charged right at them.

Hannah grabbed at his legs, but she missed. Rebecca jumped back. And they both sat down hard in a mud puddle.

"Oh!" Hannah rubbed her elbow. She looked down at her muddy skirt. She didn't know whether to laugh or cry.

"It's a good thing," said Rebecca, "that we wore our old clothes."

That set them off. They laughed until they

cried. They wiped their eyes on their aprons, smearing more dirt on their faces. That made them laugh more.

Through the blur of wet eyes, Hannah saw someone leaning on the fence, watching them. She blinked. It was another soldier, even thinner and more ragged than the last one. With him was a big brown dog.

Had he brought another letter? So soon?

"Hello, Goosey," said the soldier.

Oh, my. Hannah's heart did a flip-flop inside her chest. Could it really be?

The soldier grinned, a grin she knew so well.

"Ben!" she cried.

Chapter 3

Hannah couldn't believe it. Ben was really home! For fifteen whole days of leave from the army.

It was so good to see him sitting once more at his place at the supper table. Jonathan, next to him, kept touching his sleeve as if to make sure he was really there. Everyone was smiling, even Father, whose face often wore a worried look. And Mother heaped Ben's bowl full again and again.

"Will you have more oyster stew?" she asked. "Or more bread?"

The two younger boys hardly touched their own suppers, they were so full of questions.

"Have you got those Redcoats on the run yet?" Jemmy wanted to know.

"Did the enemy soldiers really shoot at you?" Jonathan asked, his dark eyes big in his small face.

"Quiet, boys," Father told them. "Give Ben a chance to eat."

Something was wrong, Hannah thought. She looked at Ben out of the corner of her eye as he bent over his soup bowl. It wasn't just that he looked tired and thin. What was it?

He was so quiet. That was it. The old Ben had hardly ever stopped talking and joking. And there was something else. Since that first moment outside, Ben hadn't smiled once.

Mother seemed to share Hannah's thoughts. She touched Ben's shoulder as she cleared away the soup bowls.

"What Ben needs now is rest," she said. "We will talk more tomorrow."

But the next day Ben was still not himself. He ate large plates of food and sat in the warm

sunshine, but he hardly spoke at all. Where was that big brother who used to make Hannah laugh? That strong, handsome fifteen-year-old boy who had marched off proudly to fight the British two years ago. It seemed as if that boy had somehow gotten lost and a stranger had come home in his place.

Ben was well. Mother no longer worried about that, though he coughed and was still weak. It was something else. Maybe, Hannah thought, he was still sad about Daniel, his friend from the next farm who had enlisted with him. But Daniel had died more than a year ago, during the terrible winter at a place called Valley Forge in Pennsylvania.

"It will be all right," Mother whispered to her, when she caught Hannah staring at Ben. "Just give him time."

Mother was right. Slowly, over the next few days, Ben began to talk.

He told them first about the dog, named Captain, after his favorite officer.

"He just appeared in camp this winter. We had a hard time feeding him, since we hadn't enough food for ourselves. But he cheered us up, especially when I was down with the fever. Now that we are likely to be in for some fighting, I thought he'd be better off with you. You don't mind, do you Father?"

Father shook his head. "It will be good to have a dog around the place."

Captain followed Ben everywhere. Hannah was surprised that Mother let him in the house, especially after all her spring-cleaning. But he curled up with his head resting on Ben's knee each night as the family sat around the fire.

It was the fourth night when Ben told them about the winter just past.

"I thought it could not be as bad as last winter," he began. "We were in our own state, under our own General Putnam's command. Yet, just as in Valley Forge, we found ourselves starving. Sometimes we had bread and sometimes we had none. Sometimes we had poor beef and sometimes none, and no salt to season it. And sometimes we had neither. It is a good thing armies don't fight in the winter. The enemy would have found us hardly able to lift our guns."

He stopped to stroke the dog's big head.

"How did you get sick?" Hannah asked.

"One night in March the general got word of an enemy scouting party. We were sent out to find them. We marched all night and the next morning, but found nothing. On the way back it began to rain, so we took shelter in the woods. There we stayed all night long, with nothing to eat and a freezing rain coming down so hard it put out our fires. I lay on the ground, shaking in my wet blanket. The next day I came down with the fever."

It was no wonder Ben was worn out. Being a soldier didn't sound quite like Hannah had imagined it. She had pictured him fighting brave battles with flags flying and cannons booming. Instead, the war sounded like a lot of marching and waiting and not enough to eat.

Each day, though, Hannah could see Ben growing stronger. Mother's good food, as well as rest and being at home, were making him better. After a week, his face began to fill out and he walked again with that bounce he used to have. And best of all, he was smiling.

Hannah took him out to the barn to show him the spring lambs.

"That one over there," she pointed out, "belongs to Smoke."

Smoke was the sheep Hannah had saved as a new lamb, when Smoke's own mother wouldn't nurse her. Hannah had stayed up all night feeding her, and many days after that. And now Smoke had a lamb of her own, black like herself but with a white stomach. Hannah felt as proud as if she were the mother.

"Isn't he beautiful?" she said. "I call him Cloud."

"The biggest, strongest, most beautiful lamb I ever saw," agreed Ben.

Hannah saw that old grin starting at the corner of his mouth. Yes, he was teasing her. She was so happy, she burst out laughing. Ben was really back.

They watched Cloud and the other lambs playing their silly lamb games.

"Did I tell you the story about the plums?" Ben asked.

Hannah shook her head.

"This happened last summer," said Ben. "We were camped on a point of land, and a British ship was anchored offshore. One day another soldier and I decided to go pick some plums. I was just reaching up to a low branch when the British spotted me and sent a shot my way. It missed. They fired another round, and this time their shot cut off the top of the tree. It fell, full of plums, right at my feet. Well, I picked it up and waved it in thanks. And we all, even the British, had a good laugh."

Hannah could see it in her mind, Ben making people laugh even in the middle of the fighting.

"So you see, Goosey," he said, grinning, "we don't go hungry all the time."

The rest of Ben's leave seemed to fly by. As he grew stronger, Ben helped Father in the fields and in his clock-making shop. He fixed the fence around Mother's garden and mended the big spinning wheel. He sat patiently with Jonathan and a stick of wood, teaching him to whittle.

And he and Father had long talks, their voices low and serious, about the safety of the town.

"Yes," Hannah heard Father say, "the raids continue."

She knew he was talking about the small boats that came in the night, burning barns and stealing cattle. Because Fairfield was on the water, it was easy for the British to row across from nearby Long Island, and be gone by morning.

"By the Tories too?" asked Ben.

Father nodded, his face grim.

The Tories! That was what people were called who were on the side of the British.

Though they lived here, they did not want America to be a free country, and were happy to be ruled by the English king. Some Tories helped the British, and even fought beside them. Only a few families in Fairfield thought that way. Hannah couldn't understand how anyone could.

"But we have more men patrolling the town at night," Father said. "And keeping watch at Black Rock Fort."

Ben nodded. "You must keep a sharp eye out."

At night, around the fire, Ben told more stories. The one Hannah liked best was one he had told before, on his last leave. It was about George Washington.

"Tell it again," begged Jonathan. "Please?" And on his last night, Ben did.

"We were chasing the British army out of Philadelphia," he said, "on the road to New York. We were right at their heels and got in some good fighting. Then the Redcoats turned and attacked us. There were too many of them, and they were too well-armed. We had to retreat. But before we did, up rode General Washington to see for himself. He sat on his big white horse in the middle of the battlefield, while enemy shots tore up the ground all around him. I will never forget the look on his face."

Ben stopped, and Captain nudged his knee, as if asking him to go on.

"He looked angry and stubborn and proud. He might retreat, I thought, but he would never give up. Maybe that is why, after four years and so few victories, we keep fighting this war."

No one spoke for a moment. Hannah felt as if she understood something she hadn't before. Father nodded his head, an unexpected little smile on his face.

"And that is why we will win in the end," he said quietly. "Because none of us will give up until America is a free country."

The next day Mother stuffed Ben full of good food. Like a sausage, Hannah thought. She packed as much into his knapsack as he could carry. Then they had to say good-bye again.

Captain didn't understand that he wasn't going too. He barked and tried to follow Ben. Finally Jemmy had to tie him to a fence post.

"Will you look after him?" Ben asked, his hand on Jemmy's shoulder.

"I will," promised Jemmy.

Then they were all waving as Ben walked slowly down the road.

How different it was, Hannah thought, from when he and Daniel had marched off to fight two years ago. They had been so eager then, their fathers' muskets on their shoulders, so young and strong. Now there was just one, and he was tired.

But Ben would never give up. She knew it. He would keep fighting.

Chapter 4

Captain was missing Ben. Hannah could see it in the way his long ears drooped. His eyes looked sad. And whenever anyone passed on the road, he would run out, barking eagerly. Then, when he saw it wasn't Ben, he would come slowly back to lie down in the sun.

"I know how you feel," Hannah whispered, stroking his soft ears the way she had seen Ben do. "I miss him too."

Jemmy took good care of the dog, just as he had promised. He fed him table scraps and put out water for him and took him to the barn when he did his chores. He even tried to teach him to herd sheep. But Captain didn't seem to understand. He ignored the sheep and chased rabbits and squirrels instead.

"I'm afraid he is too old a dog to learn new tricks," Father said.

The days grew warm. On the first of May Father said, "Tomorrow we will shear the sheep. Hannah, I will need you to help since Ben isn't here."

Hannah smiled. She liked helping with the animals so much more than sewing and spinning and cooking. And Father often let her, even though it was not women's work. He trusted her, she thought proudly, ever since the time she had stayed up all night feeding Smoke, saving the lamb's life.

Shearing was done every spring, as soon as the weather was warm enough. With great long scissors, Father cut off the sheep's thick winter coats. After that, Hannah knew she and Mother and Rebecca would have much to do. The wool had to be washed and combed and dyed and spun and, finally, woven into winter clothing.

Hannah jumped eagerly out of bed the next morning. She put on the same old dress she had worn to pick geese. Shearing sheep was dirty work too.

"When will we start?" she asked Father, as he came in from the barn for breakfast.

Father didn't seem to hear. He had a strange look on his face.

"What is it?" Mother asked.

Father sat down heavily in his chair. "I just saw William passing by on the road. A party of British soldiers came in the night. They broke into General Silliman's house and kidnapped him. He has been taken prisoner."

Hannah's mind spun. William, Daniel's older brother, was a member of the town militia, the soldiers who guarded Fairfield. And General Silliman was the head of the militia. He was one of the most important men in town. How could this happen? This was terrible news.

"It was the Tories," Father said, shaking his head. "They helped the British steal in and then get away in a small whaleboat."

The Tories again, Hanna thought. And most likely someone from their own town. How dreadful!

"Didn't the militia chase after them?" Jemmy asked.

"The general's brother tried to raise the alarm," Father said. "But by the time he could awaken enough men, it was too late. They had gotten away."

"Poor Mrs. Silliman," murmured Mother. "How frightened she must be."

Hannah tried to put the kidnapping out of her mind as she and Father and Jemmy went out to the barn. But it hung over them like a storm cloud. Father's face wore one of its long, worried looks. And Jemmy was scowling with anger. Hannah kept pushing back a thought at the edge of her mind. If the British could so easily come in the night and steal a general, what might they do to the whole town?

Hannah and Jemmy's job was to choose a

sheep, catch it, and bring it out of its stall to Father. They started with an old ewe, a mother sheep.

"Maaaa!" cried her lamb, thinking it had lost its mother.

"Hush now," Hannah told it, patting its soft, furry head. "Your mama will be back soon."

Hannah loved to watch the shears in Father's expert hands. *Snip, snip* they went, fast and sure. *Snip, snip* through the thick fleece, cutting it away from the sheep's stomach, then from her back and neck, legs and tail. *Snip, snip.* Father cut close to the skin, but he was so careful that he hardly ever nicked it.

When he finished, Hannah looked at the sheep, amazed. Before he started, she had been fat all over. Now she was thin, with legs like sticks and pink skin showing through the little wool that was left. A tall white pile of wool lay on the barn floor. How strange and light that sheep must feel, just like Hannah did when she took off her own heavy winter coat.

Some sheep were quiet for the shearing. They lay still, patiently waiting for this bothersome chore to be over. Smoke was like that. She was used to Hannah's touch. Others, especially the young ones, were nervous. They kept struggling to get up, and sometimes Jemmy had to help hold them still.

He was as restless as the young sheep. Still scowling, he talked all the time Father was working.

"What will happen to General Silliman now?" he asked.

Father paused a moment. "He will be taken to New York City," he said. "Because he is an officer, he will be treated well. In time, perhaps, he may be exchanged for a captured British officer and allowed to return home."

"How could those Tories do that?" Jemmy muttered a minute later. "Don't they know they betrayed their own neighbor?"

"War does terrible things to neighbors," Father answered. "And friends and sometimes even families. Hold that hind leg for me. Don't let him kick."

They were working on a young ram now. Father had named him Solomon because he said he looked so wise. He was the worst yet, Hannah thought. Every time Father started cutting, his eyes rolled and his legs thrashed.

Jemmy didn't seem to notice. "If I were older, I'd find out who they are and those Tories would be sorry." His blue eyes flashed angrily. He reminded Hannah of Ben just before he joined the army. Ben had always been angry then.

Father gave Jemmy a stern look. "Calm down, son," he said. "We have work to do."

But just as he spoke, Solomon's hind leg kicked out, right into the sharp blade of the shears. The young ram squealed. Blood fell onto the white fleece.

"Oh!" Hannah cried, startled.

Suddenly everything was noisy and confused. *"Baa!"* bawled the ram in pain. Other sheep bleated in answer, milling around in their stalls. Solomon was struggling to stand, while Jemmy tried to hold him down and Father looked for a rag to wrap around the injured leg.

"Here," said Hannah, ripping a strip of cloth from the hem of her dress.

She put her arms around the injured sheep's neck. "There, there," she said softly in his ear. "It's all right. Father will take care of you."

Solomon seemed to understand. Slowly, very slowly, he quieted down and let Father bandage the leg.

"Will he be all right?" Hannah asked anxiously. There had been so much blood.

"It is a deep cut," Father said. "We will have to wait and see."

"I'm sorry, Father," Jemmy said, hanging his head. "I should have held on tighter."

Father didn't answer. He was looking at Hannah. Father didn't smile very often, but he was now.

"Daughter," he said, "you surely do have a way with animals."

Chapter 5

"You surely do have a way with animals."

For the next few days, Hannah kept hearing Father's words inside her head. And each time she did, she smiled. Father was proud of her.

Early every morning she went out to the barn to see how Solomon was doing. Was his cut healing? Was he limping as much as the day before?

At first he seemed to be getting better. But then one morning, when the other sheep were let out to pasture, the young ram still lay in the straw. He could not get up.

Father bent down to examine his leg. "It is hot and swollen," he said, shaking his head. "That cut is not healing."

Hannah gazed at Solomon, lying there so quietly, not complaining. Only his eyes looked puzzled. *Why can't I stand up?* they seemed to ask.

She had to help him. But what could she do?

Hannah thought about it all morning while she helped Mother knead the bread for the week's baking. And did a little stitching on her hated sampler. And pulled up weeds in the vegetable garden. It was while she was weeding the herbs that she thought of Granny Hannah.

That was what people used to call the grandmother Hannah had been named after. She had been a midwife, the woman who came to help when a baby was being born. And people in her Massachusetts town had called on her when they were sick or hurt too. Granny Hannah could cure just about anything with her healing herbs, Mother often said proudly.

Healing herbs. That was it! If herbs could heal people, maybe they could heal a hurt sheep.

"Mother!" Hannah called, running to the house.

Mother was just taking the bread from the oven. She set down on the table two steaming loaves, smelling so good that they begged to be tasted. As soon as she heard Hannah's idea, she nodded.

"You know she wrote down some of her cures," Mother said. "I have a little book of her receipts."

Mother went to the small leather-covered box with the curved top where Father kept the family Bible and all of Ben's letters. She took out a thin pile of pages bound together with thread. "Perhaps you will find something here," she said.

Hannah sat at the kitchen table, carefully turning the pages. *Tock, tock* went the tall clock in the corner, the first one Father had ever made. Granny Hannah's writing, in fading brown ink, was tiny and spidery fine. Hannah could barely make out the words. And when she could make them out, she didn't know what they were. Dock root. Basswood. Pennyroyal. Mugwort. Agrimony. Wormwood. Could there really be so many herbs?

Some of them she knew, of course. *Spearmint,* wrote Granny Hannah. *For sickness at the stomach, drink spearmint tea.* And *Marigold. Brew into a tea for fever and measles. Juice of petals for toothache.* And *Feverfew. For headache, nerves, and fevers. Also eases insect bites.*

But what about healing cuts? Hannah kept reading.

Plantain, she read. *Good for healing of wounds. Boil up leaves and apply as a poultice.*

A bubble of excitement rose in her. "Mother," she said, "what is plantain?"

Mother was stirring the stew for the noon-time dinner, her face pink with the heat of the fire. "Plantain," she said, "is a wild plant. I used to gather it with your grandmother when we went out into the woods and fields. Now what did it look like? Oh, yes, I remember."

"Can we look for some?" asked Hannah. "Please?"

"After dinner," Mother promised.

So that afternoon Mother and Hannah took a walk along the road and the edge of the fields. Jonathan came along too.

"I'm good at finding things," he reminded Hannah. "Remember when I found your needle hidden in the sand on the kitchen floor?"

Hannah smiled at him. "So you did, little Sharp Eyes."

"It was winking at me," he said.

Plantain wouldn't be so easy to spot, Mother explained. It looked like many other wild plants, with broad, flat, dark-green leaves close to the ground. Its tiny white flowers, on a thin spike rising from the center of the plant, were easier to see. However, May was too early for the flowers.

The three of them walked with their heads down, looking.

"Is this it?" Hannah would ask every few minutes.

"I found it!" Jonathan would cry.

But Mother kept shaking her head.

It was Jonathan whose sharp eyes finally spotted what they were looking for. "I found it!" he said once more. "I think."

Mother bent down to look. "Yes, you have," she agreed.

"Good work," said Hannah, patting his dark head, and Jonathan's serious face broke into a wide smile.

They gathered plantain leaves in Mother's apron, then hurried back to the house.

"How do we make them into a poultice?" Hannah asked.

"Watch," said Mother.

Soon she had the leaves boiling in a pot of water over the kitchen fire. As she stirred the pot with her long wooden spoon, Hannah thought about Mother's hands. They were so small, yet they could do so many things. They kneaded and stirred. They spun and wove and sewed. They scrubbed and dug in the garden.

Busy hands. Strong hands. Gentle hands, when Hannah was sick or sad. Helping hands.

Mother stirred for a long time. Very carefully, she poured some of the liquid from the pot over a dish of bran. Then she spread the warm moist mush onto a cloth. "Here is your poultice," she said.

"Oh, thank you," said Hannah.

She almost ran to the barn. Inside the sheep stall, she found Solomon, still lying quietly on his bed of straw.

"I've brought something to make you better," she told the young ram.

She sat down next to him. Either his injured leg hurt too much to move, or he understood that Hannah was trying to help him. Solomon hardly stirred as she packed the poultice onto the wound.

"Just lie quietly now," she whispered. "Let the healing medicine work."

Twice more that day Hannah applied a poultice to Solomon's leg.

"Does it look any better?" she asked Father, as they were bedding down the animals for the night.

"I can't tell," Father replied. "It will probably take a few days till we know."

A week later, just as the sun was rising above the trees of the woodlot, Hannah hurried out to the barn. She found Jonathan already there.

"Look," he said, pointing.

There was Solomon, standing on all four legs.

"Oh!" Hannah hugged her little brother. "It worked!"

Her hands had done this, she thought suddenly. She had helping hands too.

She closed her eyes for a moment.

"Thank you, Granny Hannah," she said softly.

Chapter 6

Dear *Ben,* wrote Hannah in her very best handwriting.

She dipped her quill pen, made from a goose feather, into the ink bottle. *I cured a sheep, using one of Granny Hannah's herbal receipts. It was the young ram Solomon. His leg was injured in the shearing and would not heal.*

She stopped for a moment, dipping her pen again. Should she tell Ben? She hadn't told anyone yet. But Ben was her best friend as well as her brother.

I have begun to think, she wrote slowly, *that some day I would like to be a midwife like Granny Hannah.*

There. She had said it. Reading her words, Hannah smiled.

With a new dip of the pen, she finished her letter. *Captain misses you, as do we all. Jemmy takes good care of him, and Mother allows him still to sleep by the fire. The family is all well and sends their love.*

Your devoted sister, Hannah.

She waited for the ink to dry before folding and sealing it. In a few days the letter would be carried by Mr. Spooner, the storekeeper, when he went to visit his sister in Peekskill, on the Hudson River in New York state. That was close to where Ben's regiment was now. In ten days, perhaps, he would be reading it.

While the letter was traveling, Hannah and Mother and Rebecca were busy with the wool from the shearing. First it had to be washed in the small stream near the house. As they dipped the heavy fleece into the water again and again, Jonathan made sure it didn't float away downstream. After it dried, they picked out burrs and other bits of trash. Then they carded the wool, combing it through wood paddles set with wire teeth, until it was light and fluffy. Finally it was ready for the spinning wheel.

The large wheel was used for wool. Hannah loved to watch Rebecca working at it. She took small steps backward and forward, as graceful as if she were dancing. The wheel made a steady humming sound, like a soft summer breeze. And Rebecca never seemed to get tired. She could spin all day.

"I believe you walked twenty miles today," Father had said once, giving Rebecca one of his rare smiles, "and never left the house."

Rebecca spun and spun, and Hannah wound the spun wool into even lengths called skeins. Then one day in late June, when the fields were blue with flax blossoms, they were ready for the dyeing.

For weeks Mother's busy hands had been collecting everything she needed. She had traded at Mr. Spooner's store for indigo, which made a beautiful deep blue. All the other colors would come from plants she gathered on the farm and in the woods. Black walnut shells for brown. Onion skins for a dark gold. Marigolds for yellow. And irises for the prettiest light purple.

"It is such a hot day," Mother said. "I think we will work outside."

She built a fire outside the kitchen door, and set the dye pots to boiling. Then the girls began to stir. As with everything else she did, Mother was fussy about getting the colors just right. Hannah stirred the onion skins until her arms ached. Every now and then Mother would test the shade on a scrap of yarn.

"Is it ready?" Hannah would ask hopefully.

Mother would frown, shaking her head. "Not quite."

But finally all the dyes were ready. Now came the best part. Mother lowered a skein of wool into the indigo pot, stirred, then brought it up on a long stick. It was amazing. A moment ago, the wool had been snowy white. Now, magically, it was as blue as the sky.

Mother studied it with her critical eye.

"A little darker," she decided, and dipped it into the pot again.

Sometimes after Mother brought up her stick, Hannah or Rebecca would cry, "Oh, that is just right!" And Mother would hand the wool to them to hang on the drying rack.

Even more magical to Hannah was watching Mother combine colors. She took skeins of dark yellow, dipped them into the pot of blue, and suddenly she was holding yarn of a deep mossy green.

Hannah sighed. "That is perfect."

Soon wool was everywhere. It overflowed the drying rack, dangling from bushes and tree branches. Hannah felt as if she were sitting in the middle of a rainbow. Finally the last skeins had been dyed. She and Mother and Rebecca sat down to rest in the shade of the pear tree.

"That," said Mother, looking pleased, "was a good day's work."

Hannah and Rebecca smiled at each other. Mother always said that when they were all so tired they could barely move.

They sat quietly for a few minutes, fanning themselves.

"This old tree has given us good shelter," Mother said.

"Tell the story of the tree," Hannah urged. It was one of her favorites.

"Well," began Mother, "you know that our name, Perley, means 'pear orchard.' Your great-great-grandfather, Allan Perley, came from England. When he settled in Ipswich, Massachusetts, he planted pear trees all around his house. As his four sons grew up, they planted pear trees around their houses. When your grandfather moved to Connecticut, he brought along seeds from one of his father's trees. And the very first thing he did was to plant a pear tree."

Hannah knew the end of the story. "That was this tree. It has been here ever since," she finished.

She gazed up at its neat dark-green leaves, fluttering in a little bit of a breeze. She liked thinking that her grandfather and great-grandfather and great-great-grandfather had looked up at leaves just like these. It made her feel a part of something that went on and on.

"If I ever move away from here," she said, "I will plant a pear tree too."

Mother smiled, but she seemed to be thinking of something else.

"If you girls could choose a color of yarn, which one would it be?" she asked.

Rebecca knew her answer right away. "The bright yellow."

Hannah took a little longer. "The gold is pretty," she said. "And so is the green. But I think I like the pale purple best."

"Then those will be the colors of your dresses," said Mother.

"*Our* dresses?" repeated Hannah. "We are to have new dresses?"

She couldn't believe it. All the cloth Mother wove was always for the soldiers. A new blue winter coat for Ben. Breeches, blankets. The family had to make do with what they had. Hannah couldn't remember the last time she and Rebecca had had new dresses. Could it have been before the war?

"A new dress to wear to church," Rebecca said softly. "Oh, thank you, Mother!" Her face flushed pink and she had a faraway look in her eyes.

When had Hannah seen that look before? Last Sunday, she remembered suddenly. At church. Rebecca had talked to William and his mother for a long time after the service, while Hannah waited impatiently to go home. Did that mean something? Could they be courting?

Rebecca never told Hannah what was going on inside her head. She was like Father that way, keeping secrets. Hannah would have to watch her carefully next Sunday.

"When will you start the dresses?" she asked eagerly.

"I must make Ben a new winter coat first," Mother answered. "But you shall have them by fall."

By fall. When the leaves on the pear tree turned yellow and orange and crunched beneath her feet, Hannah would walk to church in her beautiful new purple dress. And Rebecca would be beside her in her pretty yellow one.

New dresses! She could hardly wait.

Chapter 7

A few days later Hannah sat outside the kitchen door, shelling peas for dinner. Bees buzzed in Mother's herb garden. A hazy sun burned behind the morning mist. It was going to be a hot day.

Hannah picked up a plump pea pod and squeezed it. The pod split open neatly, right down the middle. And there inside, lined up in a row, were six fat, perfect peas. She smiled. She didn't always understand the God that the Reverend Eliot talked about in his Sunday sermons. But she could see Him in her mind inventing the pea. It was one of His best ideas.

She popped one into her mouth. It tasted

green, like summer. She dropped the rest, *plunk, plunk, plunk,* into the bowl beside her.

That was when she heard the shots. *One, two, three.* They came from Black Rock Fort. Hannah knew what that meant. Danger! The fort, which sat on the coast of Long Island Sound, guarded the town from enemy ships.

Suddenly she remembered. The British had attacked New Haven, to the east, just two days ago, on July fifth.

"Mother!" Hannah jumped up, spilling the bowl of peas.

Inside, Mother stood next to the oven, her face pale. "I heard," she said.

In minutes Jemmy and Jonathan came running in from the fields, followed by Father.

"It's the British!" cried Jonathan.

"A whole fleet anchored off Kenzie's Point!" added Jemmy breathlessly.

As always, Father was calm. "We must not panic," he said quietly. "We do not know yet what the ships are doing. Perhaps they will keep going, back to New York City."

New York City was held by the British, captured early in the war.

"But if they attack us!" Mother's forehead wrinkled with worry. "Most of our militia has gone to help out in New Haven. There are no soldiers left to defend Fairfield."

"I know the danger is real," agreed Father. "Still we need to remain calm. Come, let us have dinner."

Father had a way of soothing everyone. Hannah felt her insides quieting down. She went out to pick up the spilled peas. Mother and Rebecca went back to cooking. And soon they were sitting down to dinner, just as if it were an ordinary day, as if a large fleet of enemy ships wasn't sitting offshore.

The only difference was in Father's blessing before the meal. "And Heavenly Father," he added at the end of his usual prayer, "give us the strength we need to meet the dangers of this day. Amen."

Dinner was the last quiet moment of the day. Soon after, they began to hear noise on the road outside. Looking out, Hannah saw women and children streaming by. Some were on horseback, some on foot, some pushing handcarts piled high with their belongings. They were all going north, away from town.

Hannah and Jemmy and Jonathan watched from the front door.

"We're heading for Greenfield Hill," one old woman called to them. "You better leave. The British are coming!"

But Father kept waiting for more news. Had the British left their ships? Or had they sailed on? Were they really coming?

Just after the tall clock struck three, someone came racing down the road, raising a cloud of dust. As the rider came closer, Hannah saw that it was Jemmy's friend Sam Rowland, on his family's old white mare. He was kicking her broad sides, trying to make her go faster.

"They're a-coming!" he shouted.

Jemmy waved at him. "How do you know?"

Sam stopped. "I was up in the church

steeple," he said, panting. "I saw Redcoats marching along the beach. They turned up the lane to the courthouse."

Then, digging his heels into his horse's sides, he waved and rode off.

"I must go," said Father's voice behind Hannah. "Every man in town will be needed."

He picked up the old musket next to the front door, the one he had repaired in his clock-making shop after he gave Ben his gun.

"I want to go too," Jemmy said suddenly. He stood up tall, trying to look like a man, though Hannah could see his knees shaking.

Father frowned. "No, son," he said firmly. "I need you here to take care of the house and family. I am counting on you to do that."

Jemmy swallowed hard. "Yes, sir."

Father squeezed his shoulder, said a few words to Mother, and was gone.

Without Father, Hannah thought, the house seemed different, as if it were made of paper instead of wood. Anyone could come and knock it over, burn it, steal everything they had, and what could they do about it?

She felt her own knees shaking. What was going to happen now?

She heard cannons in the distance. And, closer, the sound of guns. Father's could be one of them, firing on the British. On the road, people kept hurrying past, fleeing to the safety of Greenfield Hill.

"Shouldn't we leave too?" Hannah asked.

Everyone looked at Mother. For a moment, she didn't answer. Then she lifted her head in a way that said she had decided something.

"I will not be driven from my house," she said quietly. "I have been told that the British officers are gentlemen. They will not harm us. And we are far enough from town that they may not even come this way."

Hannah wished she could feel as sure as that. And as brave.

"Now we must prepare ourselves." Mother drew herself up straight, like an officer giving orders to her troops. "Jemmy and Jonathan, take the animals and hide them in the woods. We will not give those Redcoats anything for their dinner. Hannah, you best go help them. And Rebecca, you can cook up some johnny-cake for our supper."

Hannah hurried to the barn. While Jemmy saddled Ned, the big chestnut horse, she and Jonathan led the two cows outside.

They moved so slowly. Of course. They didn't understand why they were leaving their stalls at milking time.

"Come, Hattie," urged Hannah.

"We're going for a walk," said Jonathan.

As soon as they were moving, Hannah left them to Jonathan and went back for the sheep. But how could she get all sixteen to the woods? If only Captain had learned to herd sheep!

The dog seemed to want to help. He barked, but that only made the mothers and lambs crowd nervously together. Food, Hannah thought. That was the only thing they understood. She picked up a pail of oats and held out a handful. Smoke nuzzled her hand.

"Come," she said. "Oh, please, Smoke." And she backed slowly away.

It seemed like hours before Hannah got the sheep out of the barn. She pushed and pulled and coaxed, dropping little piles of oats farther and farther away. They refused to go into the woods, but scattered into the fields. At least, she thought, they were far from the barn. Any Redcoats who tried to round them up would have as much trouble as she'd had.

All the time she struggled with the sheep, Hannah could hear the sounds of fighting. Sometimes far away, sometimes nearer. Closing her eyes, she said a little prayer. *Don't let anything happen to Father.*

When Hannah finally returned to the house, she found Mrs. Wakefield there. She was their neighbor, William and Daniel's mother. Ever since Daniel had died, she seemed nervous all the time. She held the hands of her two youngest girls, her plump body shaking so she could hardly speak.

"We must leave!" she said. "The British are setting fire to the houses."

Mother stared at her. "I can't believe it," she said. "Sit down, Mary, and calm yourself."

Just then Jemmy burst in. "The sky!" he cried. "It's all ablaze."

Rushing to the door, they all looked out.

Above the trees, toward town, the sky was black with smoke.

"Oh, my!" gasped Mother. For a long minute she seemed undecided. Hannah could see in her eyes the need to stay, to defend their home, warring with the need to go, to keep them all safe. Then, very calmly, she said, "You're right, Mary. We must leave."

There was no time to load up any of their belongings. And Ned was hidden in the woods. They would have to go on foot.

"Mother," said Rebecca at the door. "What about the silver?"

The family owned a few silver spoons. And a cup. And a silver teapot that had once belonged to Granny Hannah.

Mother frowned. "We cannot leave it. But we can't carry it and risk being stopped by British soldiers. We must hide it. But where?"

"I buried our valuables in the wheat field," said Mrs. Wakefield.

"There is no time for that," replied Mother. "Perhaps the well."

Hannah was looking frantically around the kitchen. There must be a hiding place somewhere. "The chimney!" she said suddenly.

Mother's face brightened. "No one would think of looking there."

Jemmy kicked aside the still-warm coals and reached up to a ledge inside. In a minute the silver was hidden. Then he and Rebecca put the fireplace back in order so it looked as if it had never been disturbed.

"We must take the Bible," said Mother, snatching up the box that held it and Ben's letters.

That reminded Hannah. She had a valuable of her own.

"Just a minute," she said racing upstairs. Next to her bed was the little lamb Ben had carved for her two years ago. Baby Smoke. Clutching it tight, she ran downstairs.

Then without looking back, she took Jonathan's hand and set off for Greenfield Hill.

Chapter 8

The night that followed was the most terrible one Hannah could remember.

The family huddled together on a wooded hillside overlooking town, along with the Wakefields and other families. Hannah's friend Betsy Spooner was there with her mother and younger brothers. And Billy Partridge, whom Jemmy liked to play tricks on at school, was there too. The mothers talked to one another in hushed voices and tried to comfort frightened babies. Lucy, the littlest Wakefield girl, couldn't stop crying.

Looking down, Hannah felt like crying too. Most of the town seemed to be burning.

Orange flames shot up and black smoke swirled. As darkness fell, the blaze lit up the dark clouds above and the sea beyond. The night sky was filled with a strange reddish glow.

And then the sky began to rumble. A low mutter at first, it grew into deep growls. Then louder and louder until long, rolling waves of thunder shook the earth beneath their feet. Lightning split the clouds in bright white forks. The skies opened, and sheets of rain came pouring down.

Everyone scrambled to find shelter under bushes and rock ledges. But Hannah just stood with the rain soaking her thin dress, filling her eyes so she could no longer see anything.

This must be the end of the world, she thought.

"Hannah!" Mother's fingers grasped her arm, pulling her down under the Spooners' wagon. "It's all right," she whispered, holding her close.

It wasn't all right, Hannah knew. It might

never be all right again. But little by little, as the lightning dimmed to flickers and the thunder rolled away to another part of the sky, she felt herself grow quieter.

"Would you like my blanket?" Betsy's voice came out of the darkness.

"You must try to sleep," said Mother.

How could she possibly sleep? Damp and miserable, Hannah wrapped herself in the blanket. Thoughts whirled around in her head, of blazing houses, muskets and cannons, red-coated soldiers, stubborn sheep. And Father. Where was he now? Was he safe?

Clutching her carved lamb, Hannah said another prayer for him. And, amazingly, she slept.

When she awoke, she was surprised to see Betsy's blond head next to hers. And who were those mounds of sleeping children? Where was she?

Then Hannah smelled smoke, and she knew.

Crawling out from under the wagon, she

found Mother and Rebecca standing with the other women in an anxious circle. Following their eyes, she looked down the hill. All she could see was a dark, heavy cloud of smoke.

"It is still burning," Mother said quietly.

All morning they stayed on the hillside, watching and listening. Hannah and Betsy helped some of the small children pick berries. Rebecca brought out her basket of johnnycake. Others had biscuits and bread and cheese. At least they would have something to eat while they waited.

But Hannah could barely swallow the dry johnnycake. Dread closed up her throat as the smoke below grew thicker. More houses must be going up in flames. Was theirs one of them? Every now and then came a far-off boom of cannon, a faint crackle of gunfire.

"Perhaps the militia has returned to fight," Mrs. Spooner said hopefully.

"Oh, William," sobbed Mrs. Wakefield.

As Mother put an arm around her shoul-

der, Hannah saw Rebecca's face turn pale. So it was true, she thought. She and William *were* courting.

Rebecca said nothing, but busied herself trying to make little Lucy smile.

It was not until early afternoon that the guns grew quiet and the smoke began to drift away, thinning to a gray mist. Had the British left? Did they dare return to town? The mothers talked quietly. Then slowly, the tired little band of women and children trudged down Greenfield Hill.

"Oh!" exclaimed Hannah, as they rounded a bend in the road. Ahead of them should have been the Burton farm. But it was gone.

She blinked, not believing her eyes. The house had been burned to the ground. All that remained was a blackened chimney.

"How . . . terrible." Betsy, who loved to talk, could scarcely speak as they gazed at the still-smoking ruins. And Mrs. Spooner collapsed, sobbing, on Mother's shoulder.

Under charred beams, Hannah could make out part of a bedstead, a table leg, a broken blue-and-white teacup. Yesterday, people had slept in that bed, eaten at that table, drunk from that teacup. In spite of the summer heat, she shivered.

They walked on, past more burned farms. What about their house? Hannah thought, a lump of fear closing her throat. Was it gone too? And Father. Was he safe?

But before they could find out, they had to take Mrs. Spooner home. She seemed in a trance, unable to walk or talk. Mother supported her on one side, Betsy on the other.

As they reached town, the destruction was even worse. Shops had been burned, the schoolhouse, the courthouse, the town jail. Even the two churches. Mother's eyes filled with tears as they stood on the town green. Where once a neat row of houses had been, only four were left. This was all that remained of Fairfield.

People wandered around with dazed faces.

Some carried water buckets, still trying to put out lingering fires. In front of the ruins of his store, they met Mr. Spooner.

"Oh, Father!" Betsy ran into his arms. Mrs. Spooner sunk down on a small pile of grain sacks, all that was left of the store.

Mr. Spooner's usually smiling face looked sad and old.

"All our men fought bravely," he told them. "But even after the militia returned, our numbers were too few. And those dreadful Jaegers, the Germans that the British pay to fight for them! They were the ones who set fire to everything this morning as the Redcoats retreated to their ships."

"Our men—were many killed or wounded?" Mother asked.

"Nine or ten, I believe. Joseph Bartram, old Mr. Sturgis, and a slave belonging to Jonathan Lewis are all the names I know."

"Have you seen my husband?" Mother struggled to keep her voice calm.

"Or William Wakefield?" added Rebecca.

Mr. Spooner shook his head.

They walked so fast the last half-mile that Jonathan had to run to keep up. Hannah's side hurt, but she barely noticed. All she kept saying to herself, over and over, was *Please, let everything be all right.*

The barn was still standing. And the small shed where Father had his clock-making shop. Hannah let out a breath of relief. Then she saw where the house had been. Nothing was there but a tumbled, smoking black pile, and the tall, lonely chimney pointing like a finger at the sky.

And Father? Where was he? Except for a few chickens scratching in the yard and sheep out in the fields, there was no sign of life.

Next to the chimney, something moved. It was a man, his face dark with soot, his clothes torn. He was staring down at a round object in his hand.

"Father!" Joyfully, Hannah ran toward him.

"I couldn't save it," Father was mumbling. "I tried. William helped. We carried pails and pails of water from the stream. But it was no use."

Hannah saw that he was holding the blackened dial from the tall clock.

"It's all right." Mother had her arms around him, soothing him just as she had Hannah the night before.

"But our home," Father said dully. "It is all gone."

For a moment, it was quiet. Then, her voice soft but strong, Mother said, "No, it isn't all gone. The barn is here. The shop is here. And the sheep."

"And some of the chickens," added Jonathan.

Hannah looked at where the pear tree had been. Its leaves were shriveled and a branch was broken, trailing on the ground. But it still stood.

"And the pear tree," she said.

Somehow Mother managed a smile.

"And we are here," she said. "Everything that is important is still here."

Chapter 9

"The silver!" said Jemmy suddenly.

"Oh!" Hannah had forgotten all about it. "Is it safe?"

Father looked puzzled as Jemmy stepped over a jumble of charred wood, broken dishes, and pots. Reaching up, he felt inside the chimney.

"It's here!" His hair was black with soot, but a wide grin spread across his face. In his hands was Granny Hannah's teapot.

"Good work, son," said Father, after Jemmy brought out the cup and spoons. "The chimney was a clever hiding place."

It wasn't often that Father praised his children. Jemmy looked proud. Then, looking down, he mumbled, "It was Hannah's idea."

Now it was Hannah's turn to feel puffed up with pleasure as Father said, "That was quick thinking, Daughter."

There had been a lot of quick thinking, it turned out, when the British came. Isaac Durr, the goldsmith, had hidden watches from his shop in his well. Ichabod Wheeler had concealed his silver tankard in a stone wall. Others used hollow trees. Some had hidden furniture among the tall wheat in the fields.

Hannah heard these stories and many more when the family attended church the following Sunday. The service was held at Deacon Bulkley's house, one of the few left standing on the green.

"Our holy and our beautiful house, where our fathers praised thee, is burned up with fire, and all our pleasant things are laid waste," were the Reverend Eliot's first words that morning.

Hannah's eyes filled with tears. She saw that Mother's eyes were wet, and Rebecca's too, and even those of some of the men. It was still hard to believe that the church she had attended every Sunday of her life was gone. And the rest of Fairfield as well. Almost a hundred houses had been burned, Father said, and nearly as many barns, and just about all the shops and public buildings. All that was left were the chimneys, standing as lonely as gravestones.

What were they going to do? How could they rebuild a whole town? And even if they did, would the British come and burn it all again?

Hannah found out part of the answer after the service ended. People stood, talking about what they would do. Some were going to stay with nearby relatives. Others, like Hannah's family, were living in barns, not sure what came next. Still others were camped out on the town green. She heard old Mrs. Weatherby ask,

"And what will you do, Reverend? You have no house and no church and we can no longer afford to pay you. Will you be leaving us?"

"Certainly not," answered the minister with a small smile. "I will stay, even without pay. I must rebuild our holy and beautiful house."

At that, Hannah heard murmurs among the men.

"We will show the British," one said. "They cannot chase us away."

"I will build on my old foundation," said Mr. Turner, the blacksmith.

"I will rebuild my store," vowed Mr. Spooner, "and make it bigger!"

Betsy squeezed Hannah's hand. "I'm so glad," she whispered. "I thought we were going to have to move in with Aunt Lucretia."

Then Hannah heard Father's quiet voice. "I, too, plan to rebuild. The British will see that they cannot crush our spirits."

It wasn't until they returned home that Father said any more. They all stood looking at

the sad pile of rubble and ashes that had been their home. Hannah couldn't help thinking of all they had lost. The furniture, the beds, most of the dishes. The large wool spinning wheel, the small flax wheel, the loom. There would be no new dresses now. And Father's tall clock. She would miss its comforting *tock-tock* most of all.

But he still had his tools. Maybe some day he would make another.

"It will be difficult," Father was saying. "But I believe we can do it." He stooped and picked up a nail, blackened and bent. "Materials are scarce because of the war. It will be hard to get window glass. And iron. We will have to pick out the old nails and use them again."

"I can do that," offered Jonathan. "I'm good at finding things, aren't I, Hannah?"

"Yes, little Sharp Eyes," agreed Hannah. "And I will help you."

"I can help cut down trees for the new house," Jemmy said, his eyes bright with excitement. "And I can saw them, just like Ben used to."

Helping hands, Hannah thought. They would all use their helping hands.

"Can we start tomorrow?" Jonathan asked eagerly.

"Tomorrow," said Father. For the first time since the burning, he smiled. And Mother smiled back.

Later that afternoon Mother sent Hannah to

the garden. She was looking for greens to make a salad for supper. But when she saw what was left of the garden, she put down her basket. The lettuce was trampled, the squash pulled up, pea vines torn down. And everything was covered with black ashes. The British had destroyed the garden as completely as they had the house.

"Oh!" Hannah sighed, feeling a whole new wave of sadness.

Then, looking down, she saw a tiny flower peeking out of the ashes. It had white, daisy-like petals and a yellow center. She knew that flower. It was feverfew, one of Granny Hannah's healing herbs.

I am still here, it seemed to say in a brave little voice.

Hannah bent down and cleaned away the ashes so the flower could feel the sun.

And so are we, she thought. *So are we.*

Author's Note

Early in the American Revolution, in 1776, the British captured New York City and Long Island. From that time, until the war ended seven years later, British soldiers remained in New York. This made life difficult, and sometimes dangerous, for people living along the nearby Connecticut coast.

The British might sail up from New York City and attack them. Or they might row across Long Island Sound in the dark of night to burn and loot. They were helped by Tories, those Americans who were still loyal to the British king.

In 1777, the British raided the town of Danbury, destroying army supplies and burning houses. The people of Fairfield feared another attack like this. And in July of 1779, it came. A large British force sailed from New York City, bound for the coastal towns of New Haven, Fairfield, and Norwalk. Their aim was to destroy the privateers, small American boats that attacked British trading ships on Long Island Sound. They also hoped that General George Washington would come to the towns' rescue, and they would then defeat him.

This did not happen. The people of Fairfield fought bravely, but they were greatly outnumbered. The destruction of the town was terrible. When General Washington visited Fairfield ten years later, he wrote in his diary of the many chimneys he saw still standing in the ruins of burned houses.

General Silliman, who was captured in his own home in May of 1779, was held prisoner by the British for almost a year. He was released only after his friends arranged their own kidnapping—of a Tory judge on Long Island. An exchange of prisoners then finally took place.

A simple bread that was eaten by nearly everyone in the American colonies was called johnnycake. Here is a recipe that you might like to try. Be sure to have an adult help.

1¼ cup cornmeal
½ tsp salt
1 T melted butter

1 T molasses
¼ cup boiling water
½ cup milk

Preheat oven to 400°F. Grease a large cookie sheet. In a mixing bowl combine the cornmeal and salt. Add melted butter. Stir molasses into ¼ cup boiling water and add to bowl. Finally, add milk. Stir until well mixed. Pour batter onto middle of cookie sheet and bake for 15 to 20 minutes, or until edges are slightly brown. Cut into rough squares and eat while still warm with butter, honey, or jam. Makes about 4 servings.